MW01613504

Murder at Maple Lake
A Molly Montgomery Cozy Mystery

Tessa Aura

Contents

When city-tired Molly inherits her Aunt Mabel's crumbling bed-and-breakfast on Maple Lake, she expects dust, cobwebs, and leaky pipes—

not a decades-old disappearance buried in the guest ledger.

With her Chihuahua Mitz at her heels and a handful of nosy locals watching, Molly's "fresh start" is about to turn into her first real mystery.

Chapter 1

Welcome Home (Sort Of)

G ravel crunched under my boots as I stepped out of the car. The sign in front of the house still read *Aunt Mabel's Maplewood Haven*, its paint curling like old wallpaper. The place looked post-card-perfect from a distance—and heartbreakingly tired up close.

I still couldn't believe it was mine.

The city had squeezed me dry—the noise, the endless to-do lists, friends who thought "taking a break" meant swapping one party for another. Aunt Mabel's death had left an ache in my chest, but her will gave me the perfect escape: a chance to rebuild something that mattered.

At my feet, Mitz gave a skeptical snort. "Yeah, yeah," I told him, scratching behind his ears. "It's a fixer-upper. We'll manage."

The porch steps protested every move. The key turned with a grudging click, and the door sighed open. A puff of stale air and dust motes greeted us. "Welcome home," I murmured.

Inside, sunlight pushed through grimy panes. The scent of pine and old memories lingered. The front desk sagged under faded receipts and forgotten guest ledgers. Brushing aside the dust, I uncovered a photo of Aunt Mabel laughing among guests—her smile so alive it almost warmed the room.

"She'd tell me to put on the kettle," I said to Mitz. He trotted after me into the kitchen, where pots hung crookedly and a cast-iron stove squatted like a relic from another century. I opened a cabinet and found canned peaches whose labels had long surrendered their color. "Dinner's served," I said dryly.

As we explored, memories followed like echoes: chamomile tea steaming on the counter, flour on Aunt Mabel's apron, her voice saying everything could be fixed—with butter, or love, or both.

Upstairs, the guest rooms sat hushed and hollow, the kind of silence that made you whisper without meaning to. Only the door at the end of the hall made me pause. Aunt Mabel's room.

It felt wrong to enter, but I did. Her favorite armchair waited by the window, a shawl draped over its back. On the desk, neat stacks of papers, a few trinkets—and one drawer left slightly ajar.

Inside lay a handful of notes and an old guest ledger. Her tidy handwriting filled the margins: cheerful mentions of guests, garden parties, and scone recipes—until one name repeated. *Lila. Missing. No answer.*

A chill crept along my neck. What had Aunt Mabel stumbled into?

A sharp knock downstairs made Mitz erupt in furious barks. I nearly tripped racing down. On the porch stood a wiry woman with steel-gray hair and eyes sharp enough to cut glass.

"You must be Molly," she said. "I'm Mrs. Jenkins, your neighbor. That garden's an eyesore." "Nice to meet you too," I said, forcing a smile. "I'll take care of it." "See that you do. And keep that mutt out of my yard." She spun on her heel and marched off.

"Well," I told Mitz, "she's going to make the neighborhood potlucks *real* fun."

Before I could close the door, another figure appeared—a tall man with a toolbox and a grin that could've sold charm by the pound. "Hey there," he said. "Molly, right? I'm Jake, local handyman. Thought you might need a hand." "Thanks," I said, shaking his hand briefly. "But we've got it covered." He nodded, clearly amused. "Sure thing. Holler if you change your mind."

When he left, the house felt both emptier and heavier.

I spent the rest of the afternoon scrubbing, sweeping, coaxing life out of old wood. Mitz supervised, barking at the broom as if defending me from it. By sunset, I'd hacked back half the jungle masquerading as a garden. My arms ached, but satisfaction settled deep in my bones.

Inside, I collapsed onto the couch, stirring a cloud of dust. I picked up the ledger again. Aunt Mabel's handwriting seemed to shimmer in the lamplight—*Lila, last seen Tuesday...no sign since.*

Outside, something creaked—one of the porch boards, or a footstep? Mitz's ears twitched.

I leaned forward, listening.

The house held its breath.

Chapter 2

A Girl by the Lake

Morning had barely broken when curiosity dragged me back to the old leather-bound registry I'd found the night before. I'd told myself I'd rest, but sleep had been thin and restless—every creak of the house felt like it carried a whisper from the past.

The book lay heavy in my lap, its cracked spine sighing when I opened it. The pages smelled of dust, ink, and time. Aunt Mabel's tidy handwriting marched across them, her neat loops and underlines still disciplined even after all these years. I ran my fingers over one page as though I might feel her presence there.

Between the entries, folded slips of paper poked out like bookmarks of secrets. I pulled one free—the note that had caught my attention before exhaustion claimed me. *July 12, 1974.*

"Guest: Lila. Last seen by the lake. No trace since. Police involved. A mystery unsolved."

My heart skipped. The words were precise, almost clinical, but I could hear the tremor beneath them. Aunt Mabel had written these lines not as gossip but as a wound she refused to let close.

Mitz shifted beside me on the couch, curling into a ball of warm fur. I kept reading, each page whispering another piece of a story that didn't want to be forgotten.

"July 15 – Lila's belongings found in her room. No sign of struggle. Guests uneasy. Business suffering."

I could almost picture my aunt here—alone at the front desk, worry tightening her jaw while whispers spread through Maplewood Haven's halls. Why hadn't she reached out for help? Or had she, and the town simply turned away?

The next few entries covered the mundane rhythm of breakfasts served and linens replaced, but then came another scrawled note:

"August 2 – Police closed the case. No leads. Town whispers of foul play."

Foul play. The words thudded in my chest. I looked toward the window where the morning fog still clung to the glass. Somewhere beyond that mist was the lake—quiet, mirror-still, holding its secrets.

I kept turning pages, following the trail Aunt Mabel left behind.

"July 12, 1975 – One year since Lila disappeared. Held a small vigil by the lake. Only a few attended. Town wants to forget. I cannot."

Her handwriting had grown smaller, shakier, as though the weight of silence pressed harder with each passing year. I swallowed the lump rising in my throat. My aunt had carried this grief for decades, alone.

Hours passed unnoticed. Each note revealed some new corner of her obsession—strange sounds at night, guests who claimed to see a shadow near the water, a fisherman who swore he'd found a scrap of silk tangled in his net.

Then, one final note stopped me cold.

"July 12, 1984 – A woman arrived asking about Lila. Claimed to be her sister. Told her all I knew. She left in tears. Said she would keep searching."

I closed my eyes, imagining Aunt Mabel's kind face as she watched that woman walk away, carrying heartbreak that never aged.

The clock ticked toward midnight. The registry's pages blurred as my thoughts tangled—Lila, the sister, the lake. Why had no one ever found her? Why had the town tried so hard to forget?

I closed the book gently and set it on the table, dust puffing into the lamplight.

"Tomorrow," I whispered to Mitz, who blinked sleepily. "We start asking questions."

Outside, the wind brushed against the windows, rattling them softly—almost like an answer.

Chapter 3

A Fresh Brew of Trouble

Morning sunlight poured through the kitchen window, warm and forgiving on the worn checkered curtains. I sat at the old table with a cup of coffee and a growing to-do list. *Replace the porch railing. Fix the leaky faucet. Convince Mrs. Jenkins I'm not the anti-Christ.*

It was shaping up to be a long week.

Mitz pawed at his bowl, and I got up to feed him. That's when I saw the newspaper someone had dropped at the door. The headline stopped me cold.

LOCAL BUSINESSMAN FOUND DEAD — FOUL PLAY SUSPECTED.

Harold Finch. Even I knew the name. Wealthy. Abrasive. Rumored to own half the town and charm none of it. The article said his body was discovered in his grand but crumbling mansion just outside Maple Lake. The police were being tight-lipped, but the gossip mill was clearly running overtime.

I stared at the paper, unease curling low in my stomach. Finch's death felt like something that didn't belong here. Maple Lake was supposed to be quiet—quaint. But maybe, like the floorboards in this old house, the town had cracks you couldn't see until you stepped on them.

Sipping my coffee, I scanned Aunt Mabel's kitchen—the scuffed floors, chipped mugs, curtains that had seen better decades. Secrets seemed to cling to the walls here, and I couldn't shake the thought that Finch's death and the mystery of Lila might be part of the same story.

I picked up my to-do list and added one more task: *Get to know the locals. Ask about Finch.* If I was going to understand this town—and my aunt's past—I needed to start talking.

The bell above the hardware store door jingled, releasing a wave of sawdust and paint fumes. Jake looked up from behind the counter, all easy smiles and rolled-up sleeves.

"Morning, Molly. And Mitz," he added, leaning down to scratch behind my dog's ears. "What can I do for you today?"

"I've got a long list of repairs," I said, scanning the rows of neatly stacked tools. "Figured I'd start with screws, paint, and a door handle. Maybe a new life if you sell those here."

He chuckled. "Fresh out of those, but I can offer advice—comes free with every hammer."

"Tempting." I paused, lowering my voice. "You've heard about Harold Finch, right?"

Jake's grin faded. "Hard not to. Folks around here loved to hate him. You'll hear all kinds of theories. If you want the real scoop, talk to Clara over at The Maple Mug. She's got ears everywhere."

I thanked him, grabbing a few supplies. His smile returned just as I turned to leave—warm, easy, maybe a little too easy to think about later.

***

The Maple Mug smelled like heaven and sounded like gossip. The air buzzed with laughter, clinking mugs, and the sugary scent of cinnamon rolls. Behind the counter, a woman with auburn curls and an apron dusted in flour waved me over.

"Welcome to The Maple Mug! I'm Clara," she said brightly.

"Molly Montgomery," I replied, returning the smile. "I'm fixing up Maplewood Haven—and trying to learn the town, one cup of coffee at a time."

"Well, you came to the right place. News travels faster than caffeine around here."

I leaned on the counter, lowering my voice conspiratorially. "Speaking of news... I read about Harold Finch."

Clara's hands stilled over the pastry tray. "Ah, Finch. He made plenty of enemies, that's for sure. Some say he got what was coming. Others whisper it's all a cover-up. If you want history—and theories—try Betsy over at the heritage shop. She knows everything that's ever happened in Maple Lake."

I smiled. "Then I guess I'll need another coffee to go."

Clara winked and slid a scone toward Mitz. "First one's on the house—for him."

***

Maple Lake Heritage smelled like old paper and mystery. Betsy looked up from a stack of photographs, peering at me over half-moon glasses.

"You must be the new girl at Maplewood Haven," she said. "What can I do for you?"

"I'm trying to learn more about Harold Finch," I said carefully. "And someone named Lila. My aunt mentioned her in old notes."

Betsy set her papers aside. "Lila," she repeated softly. "Her name comes up every few years. There were whispers she and Finch were... involved. Scandalous for the time. But when she vanished, the story got buried deep. You might get more out of the folks who lived it. People talk easier when the past's been bottled up too long."

"Thank you," I said, jotting it down. "Maybe the library archives next?"

She nodded. "That's where all the real ghosts live."

***

The library was quiet except for the soft rustle of pages and the tap of Mitz's paws. Maggie, the librarian, greeted me with a smile that felt like sunlight in human form.

"We don't get many new faces digging through the archives," she said. "But you're welcome to explore. Finch's name pops up plenty over the years—money troubles, property deals, you name it."

Hours slipped by as I pored over old newspapers. Most were dull, but one headline made me pause: *Local Businessman Linked to Lake Mystery*. No details, just a whisper in print. But it was enough.

By the time I stepped outside, the sky had blushed into sunset. Maple Lake shimmered in the distance, serene and unreadable.

Mitz trotted beside me, tail wagging. "We're definitely not in the city anymore," I said softly. "But this place might have more skeletons than any skyscraper."

The breeze carried the scent of rain—and something else. A faint metallic tang, like old coins or... blood.

I shivered. "Come on, Mitz," I murmured. "Let's get home."

The town might have been picturesque, but beneath its charm, Maple Lake was starting to look a lot like a crime scene waiting to happen.

Chapter 4

Secrets in the Dusk

The morning sunlight slanted through the blinds, dust swirling lazily in the beams. I'd made up my mind—it was time to dig deeper. Maplewood Haven had too many closed doors, and I had a hunch that one of them hid the truth about Aunt Mabel's past.

Mitz trotted at my heels as I crossed the hall toward the oldest part of the house. The faded sign on the door read *Private Storage*. I'd never seen it open, not even when Aunt Mabel was alive.

The knob resisted before giving way with a creak. A rush of stale air and the faint scent of cedar greeted me. Inside, the room was a maze of boxes and forgotten furniture, each shape draped in a ghostly white sheet. I flicked on the overhead light. It buzzed, flickered, then steadied into a weak glow.

"Here we go," I muttered, pulling at the nearest box labeled *Miscellaneous*.

The contents were a time capsule of Aunt Mabel's life: photographs, ribbon-tied letters, old costume jewelry. One photo stopped me—Aunt Mabel standing beside a young woman I recognized from the notes in the guest ledger. Lila. Her expression was distant, her smile strained. Even frozen on paper, she looked like she was hiding something.

Beneath the photos lay a letter addressed *Dear Lila* in Aunt Mabel's careful handwriting. The words spoke of fond memories—and regrets. A falling out. *Unresolved issues. Disappointments.* I could almost hear the ache in my aunt's voice.

Mitz pawed at another box in the corner, marked *Aunt Mabel's Business.* My pulse jumped. I knelt and opened it. Inside were ledgers, financial papers, and thick files stamped with **Harold Finch**.

"Finch," I whispered.

The papers detailed loans, property disputes, and notes in Aunt Mabel's handwriting: *irregularities in the deal... pressure increasing... H. demanding more.* The dates lined up with the summer Lila vanished.

I was still flipping through the pages when Mitz's sudden bark made me freeze.

Footsteps.

Slow. Deliberate. Just outside the window.

I snapped off the light and crouched behind a stack of boxes, pressing a hand gently on Mitz's back to quiet him. Through a narrow crack in the dusty curtain, I saw movement—a tall figure in a dark coat. He peered into the windows, scanning the side of the house. His face stayed in shadow, but there was something about the way he moved... searching, not wandering.

The boards creaked above my head as he circled toward the back of the building. I held my breath until the sound faded.

When silence finally returned, I counted to thirty before standing. My knees trembled. Whoever that was, he wasn't a tourist out for a stroll.

I gathered the papers and sealed the box again. Whatever Aunt Mabel had been tangled in with Finch, it was still alive—and watching.

The attic stairs groaned under my weight as I climbed. Mitz hesitated at the bottom, giving me a look that said *terrible idea*. I climbed anyway.

The air grew cooler and heavier up there. Sunlight filtered through a small round window, catching the edges of forgotten furniture and trunks stacked like sleeping giants. I brushed off a trunk marked *Memories* and opened it.

Inside: photographs, letters, and journals bound in worn leather. I pulled one free and opened to a page covered in Aunt Mabel's tidy script.

"Had another confrontation with H today. He's growing more aggressive about the property. I fear what he'll do if he doesn't get what he wants. Lila seems frightened but refuses to speak. I don't know how to help her."

My breath caught. H. Harold Finch.

Every entry painted the same picture: financial pressure, mounting threats, and a frightened young woman caught between them. Aunt Mabel had been trying to protect Lila—and herself.

A creak echoed from below. I froze, listening. Mitz barked from the stairs, sharp and insistent.

I shut the journal and rushed down, heart pounding, but found nothing. Just the whisper of the wind through the old windows.

By afternoon, I'd called the police to report the stranger. They promised to "look into it," but the reassurance felt hollow. I rechecked the locks, though it did little to calm my nerves.

As I gathered the ledgers and journals into a single stack, one thought kept circling in my head: Finch's death, Lila's disappearance,

Aunt Mabel's debts—they weren't separate stories. They were threads of the same knot.

And someone out there still didn't want that knot untied.

Chapter 5

The Knock at Twilight

The last streaks of sunset faded over Maple Lake, turning the water a deep burnished gold. Inside, the quiet creaks of the old bed and breakfast kept me company as I sat at Aunt Mabel's desk, pen in hand and coffee growing cold.

The day's discoveries had left my head spinning—ledgers, letters, strangers lurking outside. I needed to make sense of it all. So I did what Aunt Mabel would've done: made a list.

I titled it *Suspects*.

The word looked almost absurdly dramatic on paper, but there was no denying it fit.

Jake—friendly, charming, helpful... and definitely harboring opinions about Harold Finch. He'd called Finch a liar more than once. And yet, every time Jake smiled, my guard slipped just a little. Dangerous, I reminded myself. Attraction could cloud judgment faster than fog over the lake.

Clara—from The Maple Mug. Her cryptic warnings about Finch still echoed in my mind. *Be careful, dear. Some debts never die.* Was it just local gossip, or had she known something real?

Betsy—the historian. Too curious for comfort. She'd known details about Finch's finances and about Lila—details she shouldn't have, unless she was closer to the story than she admitted.

And then there was the man in the dark coat—the watcher. His slow, deliberate steps haunted my memory. Whoever he was, he hadn't come for tea and scones.

The list stared back at me, half the page still blank but heavy with names.

Mitz yawned from the rug, unbothered. "Easy for you," I said softly. "You're not the one investigating two mysteries and trying not to fall for the handyman."

He blinked at me as if to say *you're doing terribly at that last part.*

I smiled despite myself, the sound of the clock ticking filling the quiet. I was just starting to gather my notes when the doorbell rang.

I froze.

It was late—too late for friendly calls. The bell rang again, sharp against the hush of evening.

Mitz growled low in his throat as I made my way down the hall. When I opened the door, relief washed over me—followed quickly by something warmer.

Jake stood on the porch, a sheepish grin on his face and a small package in his hands. The porch light caught the edges of his tousled hair.

"Hey, Molly," he said. "Thought I'd stop by and see how you're settling in. I brought you something."

Curiosity prickled. "What's this?"

He handed me the parcel. Inside, beneath brown paper and string, was a gleaming set of tools. "Figured you could use these," he said, rubbing the back of his neck. "You've got your work cut out for you."

"These are perfect," I said, genuinely touched. "You didn't have to."

Jake shrugged. "Didn't have to. Wanted to."

We lingered in the doorway, the night air cool around us. The conversation drifted—first the renovations, then the news.

"I've been going through Aunt Mabel's papers," I said carefully. "You were right about Finch. There's something shady buried in those records."

Jake's brow furrowed. "Wouldn't surprise me. That man left messes everywhere he went. But be careful, Molly. You start digging too deep, and you might not like what you find."

The way he said it sent a chill through me—part warning, part worry.

"I'll keep that in mind," I said. "Thanks for the tools—and the advice."

He smiled, but it didn't quite reach his eyes this time. "Anytime. And, hey—if you ever need a hand with more than the renovations..." He winked. "...I'm good with other stuff, too."

My laugh came out softer than I meant it to. "Goodnight, Jake."

"Night, Molly."

He turned to leave, his figure fading into the twilight as the crickets started their nightly chorus. I lingered at the doorway, watching until he disappeared down the path.

Behind me, the floor creaked—one long, dragging groan that didn't sound like settling wood.

Mitz's ears perked up.

I spun around.

The house had gone still again.

Chapter 6

What Lies Beneath

I hadn't planned on going back to the library so soon, but something about that old headline—*Local Businessman Linked to Lake Mystery*—wouldn't leave me alone. It had my mind buzzing all night. Maybe I'd missed something. Maybe there was more buried in those stacks than Maggie the librarian realized. So, first thing in the morning I headed back.

The library loomed like a sleeping relic, its ivy-covered stone and cracked windows whispering of stories best forgotten. Inside, the air was thick with the scent of dust and paper. Each step I took echoed across the warped floorboards.

I spent hours combing through stacks of yellowed newspapers and broken shelves, searching for any further trace of Finch or Lila. Nothing more, the trail just went cold.

Frustrated, I left empty-handed and drove back to Maplewood Haven. The garden glowed softly in the afternoon light, a quiet refuge from unanswered questions. Mitz bounded to greet me, tail wagging, nose twitching.

"Glad someone's happy," I said.

He darted toward the flower beds and began to dig like his life depended on it. Dirt flew everywhere. "Mitz!" I scolded—but then something metallic caught the light.

He'd uncovered a small tin box, rusted at the edges. My pulse jumped as I knelt and brushed away the soil. Inside lay a leather-bound journal and a handful of brittle papers.

The initials on the cover stopped me cold: *L. M.*

Lila's journal.

Her handwriting was neat but hurried, her words raw. *Harold keeps pressing about the property. I don't trust him. I need to tell Mabel, but I'm afraid she'll be angry.*

Each entry painted a clearer picture—Finch threatening, Lila cornered, fear creeping into every line. Among the papers, one letter stood out. *Final warning. Deal gone sour. Settlement required.* Signed only — **H.F.**

I sat back on the grass, the pieces sliding into place. Finch had been manipulating her. And Aunt Mabel...she must've known.

A rustle behind me made me jump.

Jake appeared from the path, holding two steaming cups. "Hey," he said, catching his breath. "Brought reinforcements."

Relief washed through me. "You read minds now?"

He grinned and handed me a cup. "You looked like you could use one."

Soon the journal and papers were spread between us on the grass. Jake read quietly, his brow furrowed. "This is big, Molly. Finch wasn't just ruthless—he was dangerous. You're onto something."

"I need to confront the people who knew them," I said.

He squeezed my hand, warm and steady. "Let me help you with this. We don't know what he was all involved in. It could be dangerous."

"Okay, I appreciate that." I nodded.

By dusk, the air turned cool and heavy. Jake left with a promise to check in tomorrow, and I carried the documents inside. The kitchen light pooled across the table as I reread Lila's words, the house creaking softly around me.

Then—**the doorbell.**

My heart lurched. It was late.

When I opened the door, no one was there. Only an envelope, pale against the dark porch.

One word scrawled across it: *Stop.*

Inside, a typed note: *Stop digging, or you'll regret it. The past is buried for a reason.*

My stomach twisted. Someone knew what I'd found.

I locked every door and window, made tea, and tried to breathe. But even chamomile couldn't settle the feeling that someone was still watching.

Mitz lifted his head, ears twitching, and padded to the door. A faint rustle came from the garden. I glanced out—the bushes swayed, just enough to make my skin crawl.

A shadow slipped past the shed.

I turned off the light and stepped back, heart hammering. Whoever they were, they didn't want me finding the truth. I scooped up Mitz and went upstairs to my room. Sleep didn't come easy. I startled with every creak of the house and sound of the wind outside.

Morning came pale and thin, but my resolve hardened with it. I'd been warned once—fine. I wouldn't wait for twice.

***

At The Maple Mug, Clara's eyes widened when I told her. She leaned close, voice low. "That's not about gossip, Molly. There are people in this town who'll do anything to keep the past quiet."

"Then they picked the wrong person to scare."

I left with my coffee, the warning note folded tight in my pocket. Maple Lake shimmered in the distance, deceptively calm.

I wasn't backing down. Not now.

Chapter 7

The Shattered Silence

As I busied myself around the inn, aimlessly straightening random items on the bookshelves, my mind raced with the events of yesterday. The night pressed close around Maplewood Haven, thick with the hum of crickets and the whisper of wind through the trees. I sat at the desk, the glow of a single lamp spilling across Lila's journal and Finch's letters. Sleep was impossible. The threatening note lay folded beside me like a dare.

Around midnight, the quiet broke.

A crash echoed from Aunt Mabel's office—a heavy thud, then the sound of splintering wood.

My pulse spiked. I grabbed the flashlight from the drawer, Mitz barking furiously at my heels. The hallway stretched ahead, dark and unfamiliar in the half-light.

The office door hung open.

I stepped inside and froze. Papers littered the floor like fallen leaves. Drawers gaped empty. The desk was overturned, one leg splintered clean through. Whoever had come here hadn't just searched—they'd *ripped* the place apart.

Anger tangled with fear in my chest. Someone had wanted something badly enough to tear through Aunt Mabel's memories to find it.

I checked the rest of the house—nothing else touched. The intrusion was surgical. Deliberate.

Then the doorbell rang.

I nearly dropped the flashlight.

When I opened the front door, relief and adrenaline collided. Jake stood on the porch, face shadowed by concern. "Jake, what are you doing her at this hour?"

"I could hear Mitz barking halfway down the street. It sounded urgent. Are you alright?"

"I—no. Someone broke in." My voice came out thinner than I liked.

He stepped past me, eyes sweeping the wrecked office. "Good lord." He turned back. "Were you hurt?"

I shook my head, still clutching the flashlight like a weapon. "Just shaken. They went straight for Aunt Mabel's files."

Jake's jaw tightened. "Then it's about Finch—or Lila."

"Looks that way."

He placed a steadying hand on my shoulder. "Let's get you away from the mess for a minute. Then we'll go through what's left."

His calm was contagious. The fear that had knotted in my stomach began to unknot, if only a little.

We spent the next few hours sifting through the wreckage—righting chairs, gathering scattered papers, piecing together torn notes. The quiet between us felt companionable, broken only by the occasional creak of the house settling.

At one point I found myself watching him instead of the papers—his focus, his steady patience, the way he moved like someone who fixed more than things.

"I'm sorry this happened," he said finally, setting a stack of papers aside. "You shouldn't have to deal with this alone."

"You're here," I said softly. "That helps more than you know."

He gave me a small, tired smile. "Then I'll keep showing up."

Outside, dawn was beginning to pale the windows. The chaos around us felt a little less overwhelming, but one truth lingered like smoke:

Whoever had broken in wasn't done yet.

Chapter 8

Tea and Truth

M orning sunlight spilled through the kitchen windows, softening the wreckage the break-in had left behind. I stood at the counter with a mug of coffee, exhaustion pulling at me—but underneath it all, a spark of purpose had reignited.

Finch's dealings. Lila's fear. Aunt Mabel's silence. They were threads in the same tapestry, and Maple Lake was the loom that had tied them together.

I headed back to Maple Lake Heritage to dig through the old files one more time. I wasn't really sure what I was looking for but based on what I've read and heard already about Harold Finch, my gut told me to look into the property transfers.

I spent hours paging through old town records, their edges yellowed and brittle. Names repeated across decades—land disputes, business partnerships, social clubs. Every trail circled back to the same few families. One name appeared again and again: **Mrs. Jenkins**.

The woman who'd scolded me about weeds might also hold the keys to the town's dirtiest secrets.

I thanked Betsy and headed to my neighbor to see what holes she might be able to fill in for me.

***

By noon I was standing on her porch, the scent of lilacs drifting from flower boxes below the windows. The house was neat, prim, and guarded—much like its owner.

When the door opened, I braced for another lecture about my garden. Instead, Mrs. Jenkins smiled, faint but genuine. "Molly, what a surprise. Come in before the heat melts us both."

Her living room was tidy to the point of obsession: lace curtains, polished oak, framed photographs in careful rows. She poured tea without asking, the gesture as practiced as breathing.

We sat opposite each other, steam curling between us.

"I wanted to ask about Maple Lake's history," I began carefully. "And about Harold Finch...and Lila."

For a moment she said nothing. The clock on the mantle ticked like a heartbeat. Then her expression softened—pity, maybe regret.

"You deserve to know," she said quietly. "It goes back further than you think."

She set her cup down with a soft clink. "Years ago, Harold discovered his mother had an affair. The man was Thomas Montgomery—Lila's father. That made Lila his niece, though he never could stomach it. His pride wouldn't allow it. He swore she'd never have a claim to a penny of his fortune—or his reputation."

The words sank in like stones.

"Thomas tried to keep the peace," she continued. "But Harold's greed kept the feud alive. Threats, lawsuits, whispers...it poisoned this town for years. Lila started asking questions, digging into his accounts. She was young, but clever. Too clever. And then she was gone."

I felt the air leave my lungs. "You think Harold—"

Mrs. Jenkins' gaze met mine, unwavering. "Knowing Harold Finch, he'd do anything to keep his secrets buried. Anything."

The room fell silent except for the slow creak of the rocking chair beside us. Outside, the cicadas started their afternoon chorus, shrill and relentless.

I thanked her for the tea—and the truth—and stepped back into the bright daylight, my thoughts spinning.

Lila hadn't just uncovered corruption. She'd uncovered *family*. And that made everything—Finch's threats, the warning note, the break-in—suddenly personal.

As I walked down the path, Mitz trotting ahead, one thought crystallized like ice in my chest:

Whoever was still trying to hide this feud wasn't protecting secrets anymore. They were protecting themselves.

Chapter 9

Threads of Deception

Maplewood Haven had never felt so still. The house seemed to hold its breath while I paced from room to room, my notes spread across the kitchen table like pieces of a broken puzzle finally beginning to fit.

Harold Finch's greed. Lila's fear. Aunt Mabel's silence.

After Mrs. Jenkins's revelation, the picture was clearer—but not complete.

***

Mid-morning light spilled over the papers as I read through Aunt Mabel's journals one more time. A single detail I'd skimmed before now flashed like a signal: a string of unusually large payments from Finch's company to a small business in town.

Bob Davis.

His name had come up before—small-time dealer in antiques, reputation as slippery as an oil slick. I'd dismissed him. Not anymore.

"Come along Mitz, we have a man to visit."

Mitz let out a snort as if telling me *I keep meeting all these people and still no treats from any of them.*

***

The bell over Bob's shop jingled when I stepped inside. The air smelled of varnish and secrets.

Bob looked up, forcing a smile. "Hello, can I help you with something."

"Yes, I'm Molly Montgomery. I'm the new owner of The Haven. I'm looking for answers," I said, laying a folder of Finch's transactions on the counter. "These payments—your shop was the middleman. Why?"

He swallowed hard. "You don't know what you're asking."

"Then explain it to me."

He rubbed his temples, defeated. "Fine. I guess there's no harm in telling you now, with Finch gone and all."

"Go on," I urged.

"Finch had me by the throat. Years ago, I cooked the books on some estate deals. He found out and blackmailed me for years. I paid him to stay quiet, but it was never enough."

"And Lila?"

Bob's eyes flickered, guilt shining through. "She found out about his schemes. Tried to stop him. I think Finch made sure she couldn't."

The words hit like a chill wind. "You're saying he killed her?"

"I can't prove it." He shook his head. "But Finch had rage to match his greed. The day she vanished, he was furious."

"And Finch's own death?"

Bob hesitated. "I roughed him up once. Tried to scare him off. But when I left, he was still breathing. Later that day, I saw someone else leaving his mansion."

"Who?"

His answer came out as a whisper. "Mrs. Jenkins."

I stared, stunned. "You're accusing an old woman?"

"She's not as frail as she looks," he said grimly. "That's all I've got to say."

I looked down at Mitz. "All right, buddy, let's go."

***

The pieces swirled together as I drove to the hardware store, needing to see Jake—needing something steady.

When I walked in, the world tilted. Stacked near the counter were boxes stamped with Aunt Mabel's handwriting.

"Jake?" My voice cracked. "What is this?"

He looked up, startled—and guilty. "Molly...I can explain."

"Go on, then."

He sighed. "I didn't want you to find out this way. I've been keeping an eye on you since Finch's murder. Those boxes were evidence I pulled from the house—trying to protect you. When the threats started, I thought someone inside town was still covering for Finch. I needed proof before coming to you."

I took a step closer, my voice shaking. "You broke into my aunt's office. You terrified me."

"I know. And I'm sorry. But I couldn't risk you stumbling into danger blindly. I was trying to stop whoever was after you."

Before I could answer, the bell above the door jingled again.

Mrs. Jenkins stepped inside. Her face looked older, smaller, as though the truth had already begun to weigh her down.

"Molly. Jake." Her voice trembled but her gaze was steady. "I can't carry this any longer."

I exchanged a wary glance with Jake. "Carry what?"

She clasped her hands together. "Years ago, I was involved with Harold Finch. Foolish of me. I thought I could change him. When he began threatening Lila and extorting half the town—including me—I tried to stop him. The afternoon he died, I went to reason with him. He was already injured, shouting nonsense. I pushed him when he came at me. He fell. I swear, I didn't mean—"

Her words broke on a sob.

The room fell silent except for the hum of the fluorescent lights.

"So, Finch's death wasn't planned," I said quietly. "Just the final crack in a life built on blackmail."

Mrs. Jenkins nodded. "He ruined lives to keep his empire intact. And when it all began to crumble, he took Lila's with him."

Jake exhaled, tension leaving his shoulders. "Then everything—Lila, Finch, the threats—was one long chain of fear."

"And guilt," Mrs. Jenkins whispered. "I sent those warnings, Molly. I thought if I scared you off, you'd stay safe."

I stared at her, stunned but oddly calm. "It's over now."

Outside, the last light of day slanted across the lake, rippling gold through the windows. For the first time in weeks, the air inside Maplewood Haven felt still—not with dread, but release.

Mrs. Jenkins wiped her eyes. "I'll tell the police everything. It's time."

Jake looked at me, a faint smile tugging at his lips. "You did it, you know. You finished what your aunt started."

I met his gaze, feeling something unspoken pass between us—something steady, real, and maybe just beginning.

As we stepped out into the cooling twilight, I could almost hear Aunt Mabel's voice in the wind: *Some secrets only bloom when the storm is over.*

Chapter 10

The Return

T he courtroom buzzed with restless energy. Every seat was filled, every whisper thick with anticipation. After weeks of revelations, Maple Lake had gathered to witness the final chapter in the Finch case—and to see Bob Davis face the consequences of years of corruption and silence.

I sat near the back, notebook in hand, more observer than participant now. The judge's gavel kept rhythm against the hum of voices. On the stand, lawyers traded arguments like blows, unearthing the tangled remains of Finch's empire.

The town had waited decades for this.

The judge called a recess, his weary tone cutting through the murmurs. Papers shuffled. People stood to stretch, the room filling with the low murmur of speculation. I leaned back, rubbing my temples, when the heavy courtroom doors creaked open.

The sound was sharp enough to still the air.

Every head turned.

And there she was.

Lila.

Alive.

For a heartbeat, the room forgot to breathe. Gasps rippled through the gallery, shock spreading like wildfire. She looked older, thinner, her eyes shadowed with the weight of years—but there was no mistaking her. The woman Maple Lake had mourned for so long had just walked back into its heart.

My hand flew to my mouth. Across the room, Jake stood, stunned.

The prosecutor stammered mid-sentence. "Your Honor, I—"

The judge banged his gavel, voice breaking through the uproar. "Order! Order in the court!"

Lila stepped forward, tentative at first, then steadier as she reached the front. She glanced at me—just for a second—and in that look was everything: fear, apology, courage. I nodded, letting her know she wasn't alone.

"I'm sorry to interrupt," she said, her voice trembling but clear. "But I had to come back. I heard about Harold Finch's death. I've been hiding for years, afraid. I think it's time people knew the truth."

The silence that followed was absolute. Even the air seemed to pause.

The judge gestured gently toward the witness stand. "Miss Montgomery...please."

Lila sat, hands clasped tightly and began to speak. Her words were quiet at first, then grew stronger as the story unfolded—her discovery of Finch's blackmail scheme, his threats, her desperate flight the night she vanished. She'd survived under a different name, far from Maple Lake, waiting for the day she could return safely.

Every sentence rewrote the town's history.

When she finished, tears glimmered in more than a few eyes. Even the reporters at the back had stopped typing.

Beside the defense table, Bob Davis buried his face in his hands. The judge called another recess, voice thick with disbelief.

I sat frozen, emotions flooding through me—relief, awe, gratitude. Lila was alive. Aunt Mabel's years of guilt, her endless searching—it hadn't been for nothing.

I turned toward Jake. His expression mirrored mine—shock softening into something like hope.

Maybe Maple Lake could finally breathe again.

As the courtroom emptied, sunlight streamed through the tall windows, painting the floor in gold. I lingered at the back, watching Lila surrounded by townsfolk, her voice low but sure.

The truth had been messy, painful, long overdue—but it had come.

Jake joined me, his hand brushing lightly against mine. "Looks like your sleuthing paid off," he murmured.

I smiled. "Aunt Mabel would've loved this."

He grinned. "Think she'd approve of your new hobby?"

I glanced toward the courthouse steps, where Lila stepped into the light, free at last. "Maybe," I said. "But something tells me Maple Lake isn't done with me yet."

Outside, the bell tower chimed noon. The sound carried over the lake, clear and bright, like the town exhaling after holding its breath for years.

The case was over. The mystery solved. But as the wind shifted off the water, I couldn't shake the feeling that this was only the beginning.

The end—for now.

Thank you for reading "Murder at Maple Lake". I hope you enjoyed meeting Molly and her furry friend, Mitz. If you liked this one, I know you will love "Pandemonium at the Pet Store". This suspense packed cozy mystery continues the journey with Molly and Mitz and introduces new characters of the quant Maple Lake. It's sure to keep you guessing right until the end.

Click here to get your copy of Pandemonium at the Pet Store.

Here's a sneak peek for you:

Molly & Mitz are at it again - when a handsome but mysterious guest, Max, goes missing from her newly renovated B&B without warning.

When Max checks in, Molly's quirky BFF, Lila, is intrigued. But Molly can't shake the sense of unease around him.

When Max opens a competing pet shop in the small, cozy town of Maple Lake, it seems innocent enough - until he *goes missing*.

Molly, Lila, and furry sidekick Mitz are hot on the trail.

As *strange deliveries* arrive at Max's pet store, several locals become suspects.

The trio follow the leads, hoping to uncover the truth behind Max's *mysterious disappearance*. Soon they find themselves trapped alongside him.

Max's shady backroom deals have landed them all in quite the hissing match.

Time is running out - will anyone come to their rescue before it's too late?

Click here to get your copy of Pandemonium at the Pet Store.

Chapter 11

Sneak Peek

Molly & Mitz are at it again - when a handsome but mysterious guest, Max, goes missing from her newly renovated B&B without warning.

When Max checks in, Molly's quirky BFF, Lila, is intrigued. But Molly can't shake the sense of unease around him.

When Max opens a competing pet shop in the small, cozy town of Maple Lake, it seems innocent enough - until he *goes missing*.

Molly, Lila, and furry sidekick Mitz are hot on the trail.

As *strange deliveries* arrive at Max's pet store, several locals become suspects.

The trio follow the leads, hoping to uncover the truth behind Max's *mysterious disappearance*. Soon they find themselves trapped alongside him.

Max's shady backroom deals have landed them all in quite the hissing match.

Time is running out - will anyone come to their rescue before it's too late?

Click here to get your copy of Pandemonium at the Pet Store.

Chapter One

I was adjusting to life in Maple Lake faster than I had expected. Aunt Mabel's bed and breakfast, Maplewood Haven, was turning out to be more than just a project; it was beginning to feel like home. I'd spent the morning organizing the cluttered attic, discovering forgotten antiques and old linens that needed sorting. With my chihuahua, Mitz, by my side, I felt a strange sense of purpose as I cleaned out dusty corners and polished old furniture.

It was then that the bell above the front door jingled announcing the arrival of the mail. I wiped my hands into a towel and hurried downstairs, expecting my delivery of the new linens I ordered. Instead, I found a handsome, middle-aged stranger standing in the foyer, a man with sandy brown hair and a strong chin. I knew he must be new to Maple Lake.

"Hello," I said, offering a polite smile. "I'm Molly Montgomery. How can I help you?" I tried to be as welcoming and cheerful as possible since I have had only a few guests so far under my new management.

The stranger glanced around the old inn with a mix of curiosity and appreciation. "Hi, I'm Max. Max Reynolds." He deepened his voice theatrically. "I like to pretend I am James Bond."

"Aww—OK," I smirked back at him.

"This is where you come in and say you don't think I need to pretend, and you tell me I could easily pass as James Bond," Max said with a crooked smile.

I smiled. *A little playful. Huh.* I mused in my mind. It was refreshing. He seemed to have a restless energy about him.

He was tall and well-built with short, tousled hair. A tiny scar on his chin gave him a sense of mystery.

Suddenly aware that I was staring a bit too long, I said, "Of course, welcome. What brings you to Maple Lake?"

"The ambiance and business." He gave a wink. "Maple Lake is not exactly popular. It's a perfect small town without too many eyes watching."

"What does that—" I started to say, taken aback by his odd reply.

"Actually, I am opening a pet store here in town. Starting over." Max added quickly. Obviously attempting to change the subject, he continued.

"So, I've heard this is the only place to stay in town and that you're a great host. I can see that the location here is peaceful. I was hoping you have a place open until I can get settled in town."

I nodded. "Yes, I can set you up with a room right away."

After checking him in, I walked him to his room upstairs. "Is there anything else I can get you right now?"

"No, nothing else, Molly, I pretty much keep to myself" Max added.

As he shut his door, I tried to identify what it was about him that made me feel uncomfortable. Something seemed off.

***

The next day, I decided to investigate my new visitor further and headed into town with Mitz trotting alongside. The pet store was located just a short walk from Maplewood Haven. As I walked down the street, I spotted the pet store's sign: "Reynolds' Pets and More." The storefront was charming, with colorful displays of pet supplies and toys, but there was a sense of secrecy about it that made me feel uneasy.

Through the window I could see Max was filling the shelves with the usual pet paraphernalia—leashes, food bowls, and a variety of pet foods. He was busy arranging new products and setting up the storefront with cages for small animals. As I entered, his expression seemed polite but distant.

"Hi, Molly," he said, setting aside a box. "What can I do for you today?"

"I just wanted to check out the place and see how things are going," I said, trying to sound casual. "Everything looks great. I've been hearing some buzz about you and your new store."

Max gave a small smile. "Well, I've been trying to get everything ready. Moving to a new town and setting up shop is so much work. Maybe once I'm settled, I can have a little fun around here." He said, shooting a flirty look my way. "Kidding. Or... maybe not if you are interested."

I shook my head. He was good—charming in fact.

"Definitely," I agreed. "How are you finding Maplewood Haven so far? I missed you at breakfast."

"It's just fine," he said. His tone was neutral. "I appreciate the hospitality."

Noticing that Mitz had left my side, I glanced around the store until I found him sniffing near a padlocked door in the back of the shop. As Max followed my gaze, his demeanor quickly changed. When Mitz started barking excitedly, Max quickly pulled dog treats out of his pocket and lured him away from the door.

"Well, I better get back to work," he announced abruptly, motioning Mitz and me to the front door.

"Yes, of course, I will see you back at the Haven later," I replied politely.

As I headed outside, my mind was reeling from the odd encounter. I looked up to see a couple of the locals curiously peeking through the store window. They were whispering about Max's arrival, their voices tinged with suspicion.

"I heard he had a shady business in his last city," one said. "Not sure what but seems like he's running from something to start over in this little town."

"I heard that too," the other added. "Not the most trustworthy guy, apparently."

I tried to ignore the gossip, but it lingered in my mind as I walked back to Maplewood Haven with Mitz keeping up happily alongside me. The town's whispers and Max's guarded behavior made me wonder if there was more to his story than he was letting on.

Later that day, as I was putting away groceries in the kitchen, Lila stopped by. Her vibrant personality was always a welcome change of pace. Despite the age difference, we became fast friends since her return to Maple Lake.

"Hey, Molly!" Lila called out, practically bouncing through the door with the energy of someone half her age. "How is everything going? I heard you met the new pet store guy. What's he like?"

"Oh, Max? He seems... nice enough," I said, trying to sound nonchalant. "Very flirty, charming. Although, I don't know if he should be trusted just yet. He just seems like he has something to hide."

Lila's eyes widened. "Really? That's interesting. I hope there's more to him than meets the eye. I'll sure have to check that out." Lila giggled and added a wink.

We continued chatting a bit longer and then Lila bounded off as fast as she came. Typical Lila.

***

As I finished tidying up the parlor, the familiar creak of the front door made me look up. The sight of Jake Dawson standing in the doorway immediately sent a flutter through my chest. He was ruggedly handsome, with stubble on his chin and mud-brown hair. He had easy confidence that I had come to know all too well. I could not help but notice the way his presence made Maplewood Haven feel a little warmer, a little safer.

"Afternoon, Molly," Jake greeted, his voice warm but carrying that hint of teasing he reserved just for me.

"Jake," I replied, keeping my tone neutral but unable to stop the small smile that tugged at the corners of my lips. "What brings you by today?"

He shrugged, stepping further into the room, his gaze sweeping over the freshly polished furniture and the warm sunlight streaming through the windows. "Just thought I'd check in on you. See how things are going around here."

"I'm managing," I said, though we both knew the subtext behind those words. After everything we had been through—the mystery, the danger.

Before I could say more, the back door swung open and in breezed Lila, as vibrant and unpredictable as ever. She comes and goes like the wind sometimes. "Hey, Molly! Oh, hi, Jake!" she said, her eyes dancing between the two of us. I could tell she sensed something in the air, something unspoken and unresolved.

Jake turned to Lila, his grin widening. "Lila. How's it going?"

"Busy, as usual," Lila replied with a twirl. "But I always have time to check in on my favorite people." She settled onto the arm of one of the chairs, her eyes flicking between us with a curious spark. "So, what's the plan for you guys today? More fixing up the bed and breakfast, or are we planning a little sleuthing?"

I rolled my eyes playfully. "We'll leave the sleuthing for another day. Right now, I am just trying to keep things running smoothly around here."

"Smoothly?" Jake echoed, raising an eyebrow. "With Lila around? Good luck with that."

Lila feigned offense, placing a hand over her heart. "Jake, you wound me. I'm nothing but a perfect angel."

"Perfectly mischievous, maybe," he shot back, the corner of his mouth quirking up.

Their banter was familiar and comfortable, and yet I could not ignore the undercurrent of tension between Jake and me. It was the kind of tension that came from knowing someone too well— knowing their strengths, their flaws, and the feelings that simmered just beneath the surface.

"Speaking of plans," Jake said, turning his attention back to me. "How about dinner tonight? You could use a break from all the work you've been doing."

It was a simple offer, but the way his eyes met mine made it feel like something more. I hesitated, suddenly aware of Lila watching us with barely concealed interest.

"Dinner sounds nice," I said, keeping my voice light. "Lila, would you like to join us?"

Lila's eyes lit up with mischief. "Oh, I wouldn't dream of intruding on your little date—"

"It's not a date," Jake and I said at the same time, our voices overlapping.

Lila burst into laughter, clapping her hands together. "Oh, this is too good. You two are impossible."

Jake shot her a mock glare, but there was a hint of color in his cheeks that betrayed him. "You're not helping, Lila."

She grinned, entirely unapologetic. "I never said I was trying to."

I shook my head, feeling both exasperated and amused. "Alright, that's enough from both of you. How about we focus on something productive?"

"Like what?" Lila asked, still grinning.

"Like getting ready for the evening guests," I suggested. "And then checking in on Max's pet store again tomorrow. Something about that place doesn't sit right with me."

Jake's expression turned serious. "You think there's more going on over there than he's letting on?"

I nodded, feeling a familiar prickle of something in my gut. "I don't know yet. I just can't shake this weird feeling. He seems nice enough, so I hope it's nothing."

Jake's gaze held mine for a long moment, and I knew that look of concern he had for me when I got in over my head. We had been through enough together to know that he wasn't about to let me find myself in trouble again. "Whatever was going on with Max, it's best to leave it alone, Molly." He added with that look I knew too well.

"Well," Lila said, breaking the tension with a clap of her hands. "Whatever it is, I plan to figure it out. I heard he's cute."

Jake nodded in agreement, his eyes still on me. "You do that Lila."

Click here to get your copy of Pandemonium at the Pet Store.

Thank You

I would like to thank you for getting your copy and reading my first book. It means more to me than you can possibly know. I hope you enjoyed it and I would love to hear your feedback. The best thing you could ever do is to let me know what your thoughts are about the book, my characters and if you would recommend it to others. Please click the link provided and leave your review on Amazon for me. Thank you so very much for helping me in my publishing journey. Tessa Aura

Leave your review here.

More from Tessa Aura

A Molly Montgomery Cozy Mystery Series

Murder at Maple Lake

Pandemonium at the Pet Store

Felony at the Fall Festival

Murder at the Marriage Nuptials

A Simply Scrumptious Cozy Culinary Mystery Book Series

Perished by Pasta

Peril by Pinot

Demise by Dessert

A Maggie Wright Cozy Mystery Series

Fatal Check-In

Secrets in the Pines

Murder and Memories

Buried Truths

Footnotes of a Felony

Ledger of Lies

Lockets, Lies and Deadly Pearls

<u>A Penelope Sinclair Cozy Murder Mystery Series</u>
Shop 'til you Drop...Dead
Dead Man's Hand
Signed, Sealed & Stabbed
Scooped, there it is...Dead
Life of Pie...Cut Short
Deck the Halls...Dead
Do Not Disturb...For Good

Made in the USA
Monee, IL
02 January 2026